The Tickle Tree

Written by Chae Strathie and illustrated by Poly Bernatene

meadowside
CHILDREN'S BOOKS

Have you ever been there
where the Tickle Tree grows...

...and laughed as it jiggles its twigs on your toes?

Have you sat on the back of a giant galumph

and let out a 'whoop' as you slid down its hump?

Have you scratched an old crabbysnap under its chin

or slept through the sound of a boomjangle's din?

Have you walked with a wibblebird made out of jelly

or perched on the paunch of a blubbalub's belly?

If the answer is **no,**
then you shouldn't despair,
as I'm sure that there's some way
for you to get there.

Have you leapt like a springbungle up to the stars and said "howdy-do!" to the Grimbles on Mars?

Have you wondered why horse-riding

Or played hide and seek with a luminous frink?

poo-munkles stink?

To get there is simple,
but you'll have to wait
and hope that I tell you
before it's too late!

Have you given a **moonjack** a ride   on your foot,
or cuddled a clumph   and been hugged by a **snoot**?

If the answer is no, then that's really tough luck.
Without clear directions it looks like you're stuck.

Have you danced with a **marvellous** musical **meep**
or dunked with a dennyfish
down in the **deep?**

Have you had a **pink** puffalunk's last piece of pie or climbed a free **fangdangle** up to the sky?

Don't tell me
you haven't,
I'm really surprised.

All right then,
I'll show you, but first
close your eyes.

It's clear that you're eager to get to this place.

Where snugglebugs

buzz and ripunzelruns race.

I'll show you the way, but it's not where it seems.

Through the Tickle Tree's leaves and...

...into your dreams!

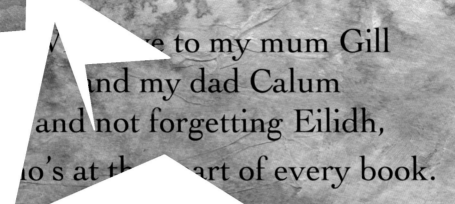

... to my mum Gill
... and my dad Calum
... and not forgetting Eilidh,
...o's at th... ...art of every book.

...ildren,

...wh... ...each... ...how to fly...

P.B.

First published in 2008
by Meadowside Children's Books
185 Fleet Street
London EC4A 2HS
www.meadowsidebooks.com

Text © Chae Strathie
Illustrations © Poly Bernatene
The rights of Chae Strathie and Poly Bernatene
to be identified as the author and illustrator of this work
have been asserted by them in accordance with the
Copyright, Designs and Patents Act, 1988

A CIP catalogue record for this book
is available from the British Library
10 9 8 7 6 5 4 3 2 1
Printed in Indonesia